Note to parents, carers and teachers

Read it yourself is a series of modern stories, favourite characters and traditional tales written in a simple way for children who are learning to read. The books can be read independently or as part of a guided reading session.

Each book is carefully structured to include many high-frequency words vital for first reading. The sentences on each page are supported closely by pictures to help with understanding, and to offer lively details to talk about.

The books are graded into four levels that progressively introduce wider vocabulary and longer stories as a reader's ability and confidence grows.

Ideas for use

- Begin by looking through the book and talking about the pictures. Has your child heard this story before?

- Help your child with any words he does not know, either by helping him to sound them out or supplying them yourself.

- Developing readers can be concentrating so hard on the words that they sometimes don't fully grasp the meaning of what they're reading. Answering the puzzle questions on pages 30 and 31 will help with understanding.

For more information and advice on Read it yourself and book banding, visit **www.ladybird.com/readityourself**

Book Band 4

Level 1 is ideal for children who have received some initial reading instruction. Each story is told very simply, using a small number of frequently repeated words.

Special features:

Opening pages introduce key story words

Careful match between story and pictures

Large, clear type

Goldilocks

Baby Bear

Mummy Bear

Daddy Bear

bed

chair

porridge

7

Once upon a time, there were three bears. And the three bears loved to eat porridge.

8

9

Educational Consultant: Geraldine Taylor
Book Banding Consultant: Kate Ruttle

LADYBIRD BOOKS

UK | USA | Canada | Ireland | Australia
India | New Zealand | South Africa

Ladybird Books is part of the Penguin Random House group of companies
whose addresses can be found at global.penguinrandomhouse.com.

www.penguin.co.uk   www.puffin.co.uk   www.ladybird.co.uk

First published 2010
This edition published 2017
001

Copyright © Ladybird Books Ltd, 2010

Printed in China

A CIP catalogue record for this book is available from the British Library

ISBN: 978-0-723-27265-6

All correspondence to:
Ladybird Books
Penguin Random House Children's
80 Strand, London WC2R 0RL

Goldilocks and the Three Bears

Illustrated by Marina Le Ray

Goldilocks

Mummy
Bear

6

bed

Baby
Bear

Daddy
Bear

chair

porridge

Once upon a time,
there were three bears.
And the three bears
loved to eat porridge.

One day, the three
bears went for a walk.

11

"This porridge is too hot," said Goldilocks.

"This porridge is too cold."

"This porridge is just right."

"This chair is too hard,"
said Goldilocks.

"This chair is too soft."

"This chair is just right."

Oops!

"This bed is too hard,"
said Goldilocks.

"This bed is too soft."

"This bed is just right."

"Who's been eating my porridge?" said Daddy Bear.

"Who's been eating my porridge?" said Mummy Bear.

"My porridge is all gone,"
said Baby Bear.

"Who's been sitting in my chair?" said Daddy Bear.

"Who's been sitting in my chair?" said Mummy Bear.

"My chair is broken," said Baby Bear.

"Who's been sleeping
in my bed?" said
Daddy Bear.

"Who's been sleeping
in my bed?" said
Mummy Bear.

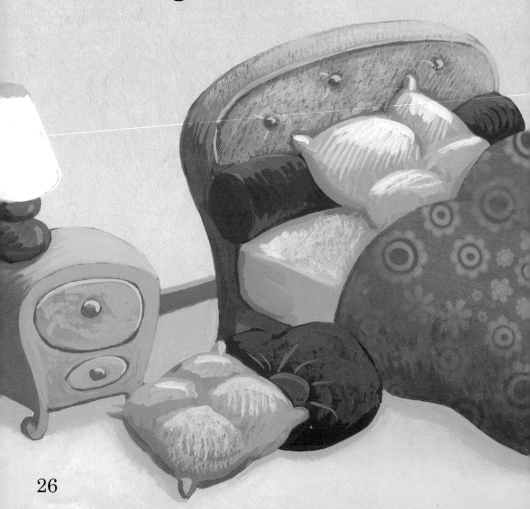

"Who is sleeping in
my bed?" said Baby Bear.

"Time to go!"
said Goldilocks.

How much do you remember about the story of Goldilocks and the Three Bears? Answer these questions and find out!

- **What is wrong with the first chair Goldilocks tries?**

- **Whose porridge is just right?**

- **Where do the three bears find Goldilocks?**

Look at the pictures from the story and say the order they should go in.

A

B

C

D

Answer: D, C, A, B.

Tick the books you've read!

Level 1

    Going Boating

☐ ☐ ☐ ☐ ☐

 At the Farm Going Swimming I am a Doctor The Bravest Fox Big Pancake

☐ ☐ ☐ ☐ ☐

Level 2

  Playing Football Daddy Pig's Office Sleeping Beauty

☐ ☐ ☐ ☐ ☐

 The Great DRAGON Party The Three Little Pigs Superhero Max The Monster Next Door

☐ ☐ ☐ ☐ ☐

Level 3

 Harry and the Bucketful of Dinosaurs Jack and the Beanstalk The Jungle Book Puss in Boots The Elves and the Shoemaker

☐ ☐ ☐ ☐ ☐

Level 4

 I am Inventing an INVENTION FRIENDS STICK TOGETHER The Little Mermaid The Wizard of Oz Snow White and the Seven Dwarfs

☐ ☐ ☐ ☐ ☐